PUFFIN BOOKS

THREE CHEERS FOR RAGDOLLY ANNA!

For a doll who's only made from scraps of material, Ragdolly Anna can be very surprising. She lives with the Little Dressmaker, Dummy and the White Cat in a flat on the fifth floor, far above the traffic, and she has the most exciting adventures.

Now she's grown to eighteen inches tall, she's trusted to do all sorts of things for the Little Dressmaker, but nothing is ever quite straightforward with Ragdolly Anna. Her balcony garden turns into a jungle, a misguided stranger hands her into a lost property office and she's nearly bought as a fairy for the Christmas tree!

Fans of the Ragdolly Anna films made by Yorkshire Television will love these six new stories, also to be televised in 1985. Earlier adventures of this lovable heroine can be found in *Ragdolly Anna*, also published in Young Puffin.

GW00728070

Jean Kenward

*

THREE CHEERS
FOR RAGDOLLY ANNA!

Illustrated by Jane Hughes

Puffin Books

Puffin Books, Penguin Books Ltd, Harmondsworth, Middlesex, England
Viking Penguin Inc., 40 West 23rd Street, New York, New York 10010, U.S.A.
Penguin Books Australia Ltd, Ringwood, Victoria, Australia
Penguin Books Canada Limited, 2801 John Street, Markham, Ontario, Canada L3R 1B4
Penguin Books (N.Z.) Ltd, 182–190 Wairau Road, Auckland 10, New Zealand

First published 1985
Published simultaneously in hardback in Viking Kestrel
Reprinted 1985, 1986

Made and printed in Great Britain by
Richard Clay (The Chaucer Press) Ltd,
Bungay, Suffolk
Filmset in Monophoto Baskerville by
Northumberland Press Ltd,
Gateshead, Tyne and Wear

Contents

*

Ragdolly Anna
and the Giant Sunflower

*

Most flats don't have gardens, especially if they
are five floors up. The Little Dressmaker missed
hers. She had been brought up in the country.
In April, when the first blossom was swaying on
the trees, she would have a far-away look in her
eyes. Then she would talk about her childhood.
She would tell Ragdolly Anna of the expeditions
they used to make to find primroses, or catkins, or
the first pussy willow.

Sometimes, when there was enough money, and
time to spare, she and Ragdolly Anna would take
a bus into the country for a whole day. Occasionally the White Cat would go too, but Dummy
always stayed at home. The Little Dressmaker
liked to take a basket with a picnic in it, and
when they came back late in the evening it would
be filled with treasures: mushrooms perhaps, or
bunches of leaves, a pretty stone for the mantel-

piece, or a branch with the buds already opening.

It wasn't the same as having a garden of one's own, but it was better than nothing. And little by little, they began to make a sort of garden indoors. At first, it was just a few pots on the kitchen window-sill. Then the Little Dressmaker found a large washbowl in a rummage sale. She dragged it upstairs and filled it with earth. Soon, she planted bulbs in it, and moss, and aconites. The White Cat sniffed it delicately as he went by. In the autumn they collected acorns from the Park, and grew tiny oak trees in egg cups. Now and then they would save orange and lemon pips, pressing them firmly down in an empty yogurt carton filled with soil, and watering them until they began to sprout.

So there was always something going on, and something to look at, even if they did live among the chimney pots. And one day Ragdolly Anna decided to make an indoor garden of her own.

The Little Dressmaker found an old dish for her, and put in a few handfuls of leafy mould. Ragdolly Anna shook a packet of mixed flower seeds over the surface. Instructions on the packet told her that they would only grow two or three inches high. Round the edge she arranged a row of cockle shells which she had brought back from the seaside. She was careful to sprinkle the leafy mould with water every morning.

It wasn't long before there was a faint speckle of green. It grew brighter, and taller ... and brighter and taller still. Then some of the little plants blossomed into pale colours – pink, and blue, and white, and purple. Ragdolly Anna put the dish on the window-sill, and the flowers bloomed in the sun. Sometimes a bee or a butterfly would come to visit them.

'They're very pretty,' remarked the Little Dressmaker. 'But what is that? There's a different plant growing in the middle of them. Come and see.'

Ragdolly Anna looked.

It was quite true. Already several inches taller than the others, the strange plant grew at an amazing speed. You could almost see it getting bigger. Before long, it was six inches high, then seven, eight, nine ... The Little Dressmaker decided it should be moved into a larger pot. 'Or it will take all the food from the others,' she explained.

The curious plant grew and grew and grew. At last they had to put it outside on the balcony. And when a great bud appeared, toppling over the guttering on the roof, they all felt that something should be done.

'I shall go and tell the Conservation Society,' said the Little Dressmaker. She put on her best hat and the coat with a velvet collar, and went.

Ragdolly Anna waited. She felt uneasy. What if the plant grew so big that they could not see out of the windows? Already the leaves almost covered the panes. Indoors, they seemed to live in a dark, greeny light. It was like being under the sea. Dummy never said anything about it, but she looked anxious. She could not watch the people walking to and fro in the street any more; she could see nothing but leaves. The White Cat regarded the whole thing with suspicion.

'It is remarkably stupid,' he mewed, 'for people to sell such seeds without giving proper warning on the packet. There should be a law against such carelessness. They should make one. But they don't. It's my opinion it should be chopped down with a carving knife.'

But the stalk was much too thick for a carving knife to go through it.

The man from the Conservation Society was astonished. He took photographs of the giant plant, and had himself pictured standing close beside it, with one hand on a leaf. Then a policeman came, and took notes with a pad and pencil, and put them in his pocket and went away again. But still the plant went on growing . . . and soon the tiles on the roof began to be dislodged, and several of them fell into the guttering.

The Little Dressmaker wrung her hands. 'Whatever shall we do?' she cried.

There was nothing to be done, it seemed. But one night a tremendous storm blew up. Wind whistled round the houses, some of the trolley buses had their roofs blown off, gates banged, milk bottles rattled, and the great flower swayed, tottered, hesitated – and crashed to the pavement.

Kerrrrrrr – lump.

Strangely, the wind dropped as suddenly as

it had risen. Ragdolly Anna and the Little Dressmaker turned over on their sides and went off to sleep. The White Cat was cosy in the airing cupboard. But in the morning he was the first up. He came into the kitchen looking important, with his tail upright.

'I have some information to impart,' he said. 'May I have your attention?'

They stopped combing their hair, and listened.

'The plant is a Giant Sunflower,' the White Cat announced. 'I have looked it up in an encyclopedia. It is an unusual variety, exceptionally large, and you should enter it immediately for the Horticultural Show.'

'But it has fallen down,' said Ragdolly Anna.

'The flower-head is quite unharmed,' answered the White Cat. 'But three tiles are missing from the left side of the roof by the chimney pot. They will have to be replaced. Fortunately, they are not broken. If my friend from next door will offer some assistance, I will endeavour to restore them.'

'Thank you!' said the Little Dressmaker, pouring the top of the milk into a saucer for him. 'But how shall we get the sunflower to the Horticultural Show? It is too big to put in any of my baskets, and too unwieldy to carry.'

'I know!' broke in Ragdolly Anna. She was looking out of the window – it was beautifully light and clear again – and she could see the Giant Sunflower in the road below. 'We'll make a rope out of sheets, and drag it there!'

'A rope out of sheets? How do you do that?'

'You knot them together,' explained Ragdolly Anna. 'I read about it in a book.'

'I don't think I've got any spare sheets,' said the Little Dressmaker doubtfully. 'But we'll go through the Rag Bag and knot together everything we can find.'

So they tipped out the contents of the Rag Bag. There were bits of velvet, and corduroy, and tweed, and muslin . . . lengths of nylon, wool and cotton. And they started knotting all the pieces together. In half an hour they had used up every bit of material and had a fine strong rope several yards in length.

'Now,' ordered the White Cat, who had taken charge of proceedings. 'The rope must be tied round the head of the flower . . . gently, mind, so that you don't disturb the petals.'

They hurried downstairs, and outside . . . 'Gently . . . let *me* do it.' He was clever with

his paws, and having looped the rope round the petals, he arranged them in a graceful manner and they set off, one behind the other, dragging the Giant Sunflower after them.

Dummy watched them go.

Luckily the Horticultural Show was in the local hall, only a few steps up the next road, so they had not too far to walk. The Judge was already making awards as they arrived, rather warm and dishevelled after their journey.

'Excuse me,' ventured the Little Dressmaker.

'Yes?' questioned the Judge, raising one eyebrow.

'We would like to enter a candidate for the Sunflower Competition.'

'Where *is* it, my good lady?'

'Excuse me, your Worship. It's outside. We can't get it through the door without damaging the petals. It's too big.'

'Too big?' He raised the other eyebrow. 'Let me see . . . Let me see . . . Just outside the door, did you say?

'My *goodness*!' The Judge drew in his breath. 'Do you know what you have got there, madam?'

'Well, sir . . .'

'That is the most splendid example of a Giant Sunflower that I have ever encountered. Quite outstanding. It must be photographed. It must be measured. It must be dried, and exhibited in the Natural History Museum. Who is the grower of this magnificent specimen?'

'I grew it,' said Ragdolly Anna.

'You did, young lady? Then I have the honour to present you with this certificate:

GROWER OF THE FINEST SUNFLOWER
(an award for Good Gardening)

And a five-pound note.'

'Three cheers for Ragdolly Anna! Hip . . . hip . . . Hooray!'

Ragdolly Anna had never been cheered before. She would have blushed, only as she was not *quite* human, she did not know how to. But she was very proud of the certificate, and long, long afterwards, when she was quite an elderly rag dolly, she would unroll it and show it to people. The Little Dressmaker was pleased, too.

'Because it shows you can grow all sorts of things,' she explained, as they walked home, leaving the Sunflower behind them, 'even though you do live five floors up. A little water . . . a little sun . . . a little attention . . . Who knows what may come up?'

'What comes up depends entirely on what you put *in*,' snapped the White Cat. 'Next time, I suggest you question the shopkeeper more carefully. Why, you might find yourself with no chimneys, as well as no tiles!'

The five-pound note they put away carefully, in a box on the mantelpiece with two rubber bands, a safety pin, and a small piece of Plasticine.

'Then we shall know where it is,' said the Little Dressmaker.

'And I'll tell you what we'll do,' she added. 'In August we'll go for a whole day in the country. We'll take a picnic, and look at the flowers, and perhaps take a punt up the river, if it is a fine day. You never know what will happen in August, and it's time we had a Celebration.

'How about *that*?'

Ragdolly Anna
is Lost

*

The Little Dressmaker was making a wedding dress. Dummy stood in the centre of the room for a fitting. She wore a wreath of orange blossom on her head, and a muslin veil. White, shiny material hung round her in folds, and she had been wound so thin that her waist did not measure more than 22 inches. She had a bright, starry look in her eyes; you might have believed she was a real bride if it were not for the pins which stuck out from her breast and hips. The Little Dressmaker was crouched on hands and knees tacking up the hem.

Ragdolly Anna watched. She hoped she would be a bride one day. But not yet. She wasn't big enough, or old enough; and it was awkward being only *nearly* human. She liked holding the pincushion, and passing the Little Dressmaker a pin when she had used up all the ones that were jutting from her mouth. Ragdolly Anna knew that she herself must never, *never* put a pin in her mouth, for fear that she might swallow it.

At last the fitting was completed. Together, they helped Dummy out of her regalia, and the Little Dressmaker sat down by the table to finish things off. For some moments she stitched away briskly, without speaking. Then:

'Drat!' she exclaimed.

'What's the matter?'

'I've come to the end of my thread. I've not a scrap left. Look through my basket please, Ragdolly Anna, and see if there's a white reel.'

Ragdolly Anna looked. There were all sorts of coloured cottons in the basket: scarlet, pink, purple, orange, yellow, cream, brown and apricot. There were a number of different greens which were pretending to be blue and a number of different blues that were almost green. There was a black reel, a brown one, and a sort of khaki colour labelled BUTTON THREAD.

But there wasn't a white one.

'What a nuisance!' sighed the Little Dressmaker. 'I was sure there was another, somewhere. I'll have to buy one, that's all. Could you put on your shawl, love, and run along to the draper's for me? The one on the corner? It isn't far.'

'I'd go with you,' said the White Cat, lazily stretching himself, 'but I have much more important matters to attend to.'

Ragdolly Anna didn't mind. She had often run errands for the Little Dressmaker.

The Little Dressmaker gave her a purse with a fifty-pence piece in it, and reminded her to be sure and count the change.

'And don't be long,' she added, 'for I want to finish the wedding dress this evening. It must be delivered tomorrow, or it will be too late.'

Ragdolly Anna slid down the banisters, as she frequently did when they were in a hurry. She had become good at sliding, and always went slowly round the last corner and climbed off gracefully at the bottom. Outside the door she turned and glanced up at the Flat on the Fifth Floor. She could just see the top of Dummy's head, and the White Cat staring from the rail of the balcony. 'Look where you're going,' he advised, 'and don't get lost. I expect my friend Professor Purrkins today.'

The draper's shop was only a few yards down the road. Ragdolly Anna remembered the way perfectly, because she had often been there before. She liked to look at the stand of coloured ribbons, the table where remnants were offered for sale at half price, and the big glass case full of sewing thread of every imaginable colour. At the end of a long line of cream reels, there was one of pure white.

The shop lady reached it down for her. She knew Ragdolly Anna well, and gave her the change one bit at a time so that it was easy to count.

'Your hat looks *very* pretty this morning!' she commented, opening the door.

'I sewed some more roses on,' explained Ragdolly Anna. 'New ones. A lot.' She had cut them out of pink lavatory paper, gathered them into buds and blossoms, and stitched them all over the crown of her hat. Each rose had a large number of petals, as many as she could manage, and the result was really splendid.

The shop door shut behind her. Ragdolly Anna paused to look in the window before starting for home. She saw the reflection of a rag dolly looking back. A rag dolly with a huge and beautiful hat ...

If she had run off that very minute without delay, there wouldn't have been any trouble. But as she stayed to admire her reflection, pressing her nose against the pane, a large figure appeared behind her.

'A rag dolly!' muttered a voice in surprise. 'Somebody must have dropped it. What a waste of a good dolly. I'd better take it to the Lost Property counter.' And to Ragdolly Anna's dismay, a great hand wearing a leather glove picked her up, pushed her well down at the bottom of a shopping trolley, and wheeled her off!

'Let me out!' shouted Ragdolly Anna. But her voice was muffled by so many brown paper bags, bundles of bananas, potato crisps and cornflakes that nobody heard her cry. The shopping trolley was jerked along at a great pace. It was made of basket straw, luckily, so that she could put her face close to the cracks in the straw and catch brief visions of this and that – flicks of light, bits of a lamp post, squares of stone wall. But she very soon realized that the road was quite new to her. How would she find her way back?

'I ought to be scattering a trail,' thought Ragdolly Anna tearfully, 'like the Babes in the Wood. But what can I scatter? I haven't any crumbs.'

Suddenly, she had an idea. Why hadn't it occurred to her before? ROSE PETALS! She would take the rose petals off her hat, one by one, and push them through the gaps in the side of the trolley. The petals would make a trail . . . and maybe, at last, somebody would come to look for her . . .

It was quite a problem removing her hat in such crowded circumstances, but she persevered; and once it was off, she was able to detach the rose petals without difficulty. She stuffed them through the holes in the trolley one by one, and watched anxiously as they trickled on to the pavement. Soon, there was a long pink trail of paper rose petals up this street and down that ... all the way to the Post Office.

The Lost Property counter was just inside the cage where they sold stamps. There were a few things already waiting there – 'hoping to be found, I suppose,' sniffed Ragdolly Anna as she

was placed among them. There was a leather purse, a packet of cigarette cards, an umbrella, and a teddy with one eye.

'What a fine rag dolly!' exclaimed the Post Office assistant. 'Somebody must be looking for her *everywhere*.'

'I belong to the Little Dressmaker. I want to go home!' protested Ragdolly Anna.

'Listen to that! It can even talk! What a marvel!' cried the stamp lady. She pulled the wire cage securely down in front, and returned to her stamps. 'Twelve at sixteen p?' she asked pleasantly. 'That will be £1 and 92 pence.'

Time passed. A great many customers came to the Post Office. Some of them looked at Ragdolly Anna, but none of them recognized her. The clock struck ten . . . then eleven . . . and then twelve . . .

'We close for lunch at one,' announced the stamp lady, turning the last customer away, and following her to the door.

She locked it, firmly.

'Open again at 2.30,' she explained.

'But I shan't get home for dinner!' Ragdolly Anna wiped her eyes on the fringe of her shawl. She felt too upset to look for a handkerchief.

'Won't you?' inquired a deep, throaty voice, kindly. 'We'll see about that!'

A soft, dark body reared up from under the counter. Then a soft white one.

It was the White Cat's friend Professor Purrkins – *and* the White Cat himself!

'Oh!' sighed Ragdolly Anna in relief. 'I *am* glad to see you. How did you manage to find me?'

'A little purrrspicacity,' drawled Professor Purrkins.

'It's what we call "deduction",' broke in the White Cat, waving his tail. 'My friend Professor Purrkins witnessed the *whole episode*,' he explained in a whisper. 'It's his visiting day, you see. He was coming along the main street from the station when he noticed a shopping trolley shedding rose petals . . .'

'*That's* odd, I thought,' interrupted Professor Purrkins. His eyes narrowed into slits.

The two cats continued, both talking at the same time:

'The rest was easy . . .'

'A case of taking thought . . .'

'And taking action . . .'

'No *wondering*, you understand.'

'You make up your mind what to do . . .'

'And you *do* it.'

'Miaouw!'

'Put those cats out, Maisie!' called a voice from

the back of the Post Office. 'What a noise they do make! Where have they come from?'

'They must have run in at the parcels door, with the postman. I'll open the window.' Maisie threw up the sash. 'Why! They've gone already! And they've taken the rag dolly with them. Imagine *that*!'

'What an *extraordinary* thing!'

The two cats had sidled in with the postman. They had equipped themselves with a long, bristly piece of string – almost as thick as a rope – so they were well prepared to organize a rescue. Once on the counter, it was a straightforward matter to knot the string around Ragdolly Anna's waist, haul her up ... through ... and out of the window to freedom. In the Post Office backyard, all three of them ran as fast as they could. They didn't go along the main road, of course, because people might have chased after them ... but through gardens and alleys, tunnels and drainpipes and chimney pots and toolsheds, till they reached their own front door.

'It wouldn't do to enter by the balcony,' said Professor Purrkins, breathlessly. 'Not with Ragdolly Anna. Even with the parcel string, she might fall.'

So they all scrambled into the lift. Luckily, for once it was working.

The Little Dressmaker was getting anxious. She had cooked the dinner, and something was beginning to stick to the bottom of a saucepan. There was a strong – a *very* strong – smell of fish pie.

They were only just in time.

'You *do* look a mess!' she exclaimed. 'You're covered with soot and cobwebs, Ragdolly Anna! But never mind. It will all brush off. And at least you're safe. Have you remembered the cotton?'

She had. It had been wrapped up safely in her pocket all the time.

They all talked with their mouths full, as they set to work on the fish pie. The Little Dressmaker threw up her hands in horror when she heard what had happened, and was obliged to take a drink of cold water.

'You might not have been discovered for *at least* a week,' she said. 'Not everybody knows that you are nearly human, you see. They would have left you there with the purse, and the umbrella, the cigarette cards, and the teddy with one eye. Dallying by shop windows is *dangerous*. Don't ever let me hear of such a thing again!'

Ragdolly Anna promised that she would be more careful next time. 'But my hat looked so pretty, in the reflection,' she explained. 'And now there are hardly any roses left!'

The hat certainly was rather dishevelled. 'It does need a bit of fresh trimming,' agreed the Little Dressmaker. 'Just wait until I've finished the wedding dress, and we'll see what can be done.'

She worked hard all the rest of that day, and by evening she had put in the last stitch. It was a beautiful dress. She had embroidered a circle of tiny daisies round the neck, and secretly Ragdolly Anna thought that nobody could look so lovely as Dummy in it. But in the morning they would take it off, fold it with layers and layers of tissue paper and pack it in a big cardboard box for urgent delivery.

For a good hour after Ragdolly Anna had gone to bed, the Little Dressmaker sat under the light with her glasses on, making a new bunch of paper roses. I don't think anybody saw her, except Dummy. Professor Purrkins and the White Cat were out on the balcony, singing to the moon.

'They may call it singing,' said the Little Dressmaker to herself. 'I don't. But we cannot all be musical. There!'

She held up Ragdolly Anna's hat, and turned it round carefully. 'It is as good as new!'

There wasn't room for even one more rose!

Ragdolly Anna
and the Scarecrow

*

Ragdolly Anna was practising her writing. She had found a pencil with a sharp point that came out black and clear, and a piece of paper from the Little Dressmaker's shopping pad. Writing was difficult. She stuck out her tongue in an effort to get the letters to stand up properly, and started with a capital A.

'Addition. A part of Arithmetic.
'Afghanistan. A country.
'Agrimony. A herb.
'Allotment. A patch of ground which may be required for horticulture,'
dictated the White Cat.

They were terribly long words. When she had reached the end of 'horticulture', Ragdolly Anna took a deep breath, and looked up.

'What's horticulture?'

'You ought to remember *that*!' said the White

Cat. 'We took the Giant Sunflower to the HORTICULTURAL Show! It's a waste of time trying to teach *some* people!'

'It's only gardening,' explained the Little Dressmaker kindly. She was machining, and had to raise her voice because of the noise. Then she paused for a minute to thread a new piece of cotton through the needle's eye. 'People usually grow vegetables in allotments. And that gives me an idea. There's one vacant, I believe, in that patch at the recreation ground, next to the pavilion. We must go and see.'

She finished her work, and folded it neatly. Dummy watched with approval. She was always glad when the fittings were over, and the dress – or petticoat – or whatever it was – nicely completed. And she didn't mind being left alone in the flat five floors up when Ragdolly Anna and the Little Dressmaker went out.

Ragdolly Anna couldn't talk much on their way to the recreation ground, because she had to move her legs so fast to keep up. Round the back of the pavilion they stopped, and looked. There were the allotments: a square field of them.

'There must be eight, all told,' decided the Little Dressmaker. 'And they're all planted and cared for except one. That's sure to be the one that doesn't belong to anybody.'

They walked up and down the narrow bit of path between the beds, and admired them. Some had rows of cabbages, and some had potatoes . . . some had lettuces and tall trellises of runner beans. One or two had sweet peas among the vegetables. Ragdolly Anna liked these best, because of the smell.

The patch next to the vacant one had a strange thing standing in the middle of it. It looked like a man – yet it wasn't a man. It never moved, except to flap a little when the breeze caught it, and it only had one leg.

'It's a scarecrow,' explained the Little Dress-maker. 'You don't have to be frightened. It won't do you any harm. They put it there to keep the birds away – stop them swallowing the seeds or pecking the raspberries.' She looked thoughtful. 'We'll write a letter to the Council this evening,' she said at last. 'We'll put in an application.'

'Application . . . Application . . .' Ragdolly Anna sang, under her breath, all the way home. She wasn't sure what it meant, but it sounded important.

That night they wrote their letter, while the White Cat reminded them that the address should be on the top right-hand corner, and the date underneath.

'Day, month, and year,' he instructed. 'That is how things should be done.'

Ragdolly Anna licked the stamp. It had a picture of butterflies on it, as well as of the Queen, so it was rather special.

The White Cat volunteered to post it. He found it quite easy to leap on to the top of the pillar box, lean over, and slip the letter inside.

In three days they had an answer.

They all gathered round to hear what it said.

The Little Dressmaker put on her glasses; then she looked up. 'It's all right!' she cried in excitement. 'We can have it. It's ours!'

Ragdolly Anna clapped her hands. (They made a soft, stuffy sound when they came together because after all she was only sewn out of rags; but it didn't matter.) They made up their minds to set to work as soon as possible, while the weather was fine.

First, the ground had to be well weeded. That was hard work.

It looked greatly improved when they had finished. Then the Little Dressmaker turned over the soil with a fork 'to let the air in'. After that, it was only a matter of planting out. The White Cat accompanied them to the seed shop, and helped them choose a packet of this and a packet of that, including one of catmint.

'Not for eating,' he explained. 'For sitting in – or under – or near. It's for Me.'

They bought a ball of string to help get the rows straight. The White Cat held one end, and Ragdolly Anna held the other, while the Little Dressmaker walked slowly along the length of string scattering seeds as she went.

'I do hope the birds won't eat them,' she said anxiously. 'Perhaps that scarecrow in the next patch will keep them away.'

Ragdolly Anna did not think the scarecrow *would* keep the birds away, for he had a robin's nest in the seat of his trousers. She felt sorry for him, standing there alone, day after day, on his single wooden leg. And one afternoon, just as they were packing up to go home, she heard him sneeze.

That night rain came. She lay awake, listening to the soft tumble on the roof, the plash in the gutter. It was a lovely sound, when you were snug and warm and dry inside.

But what about Mr Scarecrow? He would get *terribly* wet. She hoped he would not catch a cold – he had sneezed in the allotment today. She felt uneasy, and woke up several times, thinking about him.

36

In the morning, the Little Dressmaker said she had been a fidget. 'Nothing but tossing and turning. What is the matter with you?' she asked. 'Perhaps you are sickening for something. I shall take your temperature.'

She searched for her thermometer and found it, at last, in the bowl with the sticky tape and drawing pins and envelope stickers. Ragdolly kept it in her mouth, obediently, for three minutes ('Just like a boiled egg!' she thought), but she was glad to hear that it was perfectly normal.

'A sharp walk to the allotments will do you good,' suggested the Little Dressmaker. 'Oh, dear. It's still raining. Never mind. We'll put on our mackintoshes and boots.'

They wrapped themselves up warmly against the weather. Just as they were setting off, Ragdolly Anna paused.

'Wait a minute –' she cried excitedly. 'I've had an idea. A plastic carrier bag!'

'A plastic *carrier* bag? What are you thinking about?' The Little Dressmaker stood with her hand on the door. 'I *have* got one – but why do you want it?'

'To make a waterproof cape for Mr Scarecrow. We could fasten it round his shoulders. With string. It would keep him dry when it

38

rains ...' Ragdolly Anna spoke in breathless jerks. They paused for a minute or two, found the bag, split it carefully down the sides, and spread it out. It would make an excellent cape, with a bit of ribbon fixed on to each corner to tie at the neck. Ribbon would be smarter than string. It would look quite decorative. The Little Dressmaker said it was a sensible idea, and produced two lengths of ribbon, one green and one red, which would do beautifully. She sewed them on firmly, so that they would not come off with a sudden gust of wind. When the cape was finished, they rolled it up smoothly and set out for the allotments.

'Such concern! And for a scarecrow!' scoffed the White Cat. 'Still, if he hasn't sense enough to sleep indoors, it is wise to take precautions. I always take precautions myself, indoors and out, whatever the weather. Always.' He stared out of the window at the Little Dressmaker and Ragdolly Anna until they disappeared round the corner. Then he yawned, stretched, curled his tail round until it covered the tip of his nose, and fell asleep.

Ragdolly Anna could hear Mr Scarecrow sneezing from quite a long way off. He certainly had a cold – a bad one, from the sound of it.

'You ought to be in bed,' ventured Ragdolly

Anna, spreading the cape round his shoulders and tying up the ribbon bow. 'Not standing out in a downpour.'

She hadn't expected Mr Scarecrow to answer, and was surprised when a thick, soft, rather musty voice floated out of the wrappings.

'Scarecrows never go to bed, Miss, see?' said the voice. 'Scarecrows haven't got no beds. Only flower beds, see?' He gave a hoarse laugh. 'You've got to laugh, haven't you? It's a joke. *Flower* beds . . . and *vegetable* beds, see?'

The Little Dressmaker was looking closely at the wet ground, hoping to discover that some

of the seeds had come up already. I don't think she heard what Mr Scarecrow was saying. After clearing his throat and sneezing once or twice, so that a robin flew out of the seat of his trousers with a flutter, he went on:

'It's very kind of you, Miss, to take the trouble. Very kind, I'm sure. It's not many as would bother themselves about a scarecrow. That's fine, that is.'

He glanced down at the cape with his crooked eye, and Ragdolly Anna noticed that he hadn't a single hair on his head. In fact, it looked uncommonly like a turnip, only she didn't say so, for fear of hurting his feelings.

He could do with a hat, too. She herself was wearing her straw hat with the paper roses, and a plastic bonnet on top to keep the roses dry. Mr Scarecrow looked at it admiringly.

'It's a nice hat,' he muttered hoarsely. 'Now, if I had a hat, things would be better. You couldn't ask more than that, now, could you? Not if you was a scarecrow. If you know what I mean . . .'

He swayed a little on his single wooden leg. Ragdolly Anna stepped backwards. It was time to go home. The rain was lessening, and a watery sun glimmered through a break in the cloud. It was as shiny as tin.

'Of *course*!' she gasped. 'He can have a TIN hat! That would be useful in bad weather, and if it had a hinged lid he could pull the lid down over his eyes in front to keep the sun off.'

As they turned to go, she didn't hear Mr Scarecrow say goodbye. I expect he was afraid the Little Dressmaker might notice him. Scarecrows are not expected to make conversation. It might have alarmed her.

Ragdolly Anna was quiet on the way home. She was thinking about tins. There was the Button Tin, the Tea Tin, the Biscuit Tin, the Treacle Tin, the Tin for Nails, the Tin for Used Stamps, and the Tin for putting any odd things in which hadn't got a tin to themselves. None of those could be spared. She would look in the cupboard under the staircase on the fifth floor. That was filled, chock-a-block, with all sorts of peculiar objects. There might easily be a tin among them.

It was dark in the cupboard, and cobwebby. She brought out an old tennis racquet with a broken string, and four golf balls which the Little Dressmaker had picked up on the Links once, when she was on holiday; further back was a pile of picture frames – Ragdolly Anna fell over them and hurt her ankle, but it was too dark to make a fuss. There was a mousetrap . . . a box of Christmas decorations . . . a huge pile of old electricity bills . . . and a TIN. Yes. Right at the very bottom of the cupboard was a tin with a hinged lid, and a picture of snowdrops painted on it.

It would be just the thing for Mr Scarecrow.

'You *are* in a mess!' The Little Dressmaker looked at her critically, needle in hand. 'Ask the White Cat to give you a brush down.'

'Huh!' exclaimed the White Cat. 'It's time she learned to brush herself. But of course, she's not even human yet. If she were a kitten, she would have learned *long* ago. I'll give directions, if you like.'

He sat bolt upright, mewing, 'Up . . . down . . . to the right . . . a little to the left . . . now repeat . . .' while Ragdolly Anna struggled with the clothes-brush. She was anxious to visit Mr Scarecrow again without delay, taking the tin hat with her. He would certainly be pleased. Why, who had ever seen a scarecrow wearing a tin hat? He would probably be the only one with such headgear in the entire country. Perhaps even in the world.

The Little Dressmaker was too busy to go to the allotments again that day, or even the day after. There were a hundred and fifty hooks and eyes to be sewn on to a ball dress. It took a long time. But by Saturday afternoon she had finished the last one, so off they went, taking a fork and trowel for weeding, a biscuit each, wrapped in silver paper, for their tea, and the tin with the snowdrops on it.

'I'll have to give him his new hat when the Little Dressmaker isn't listening,' decided Ragdolly Anna. 'In case he says something. She might be alarmed.'

She waited until the Little Dressmaker was busying herself at the very end of the row. There were radishes there. Some of them would be almost ready to eat.

'Thought you weren't never coming back, see?' whispered Mr Scarecrow. 'Thought you'd gone for a soldier, like. Me cold's snuffed it. What do you think of that? It was the cape that done it.'

'I've brought you a hat,' ventured Ragdolly Anna. She held it up for him to see, and his crooked eye glistened.

'Snowdrops, eh? My favourites. I shall look a swell, shan't I?' He began to shake with laughter. Ragdolly Anna was afraid he might topple over.

'Be careful!' she warned. 'Keep still. I'll put it on for you.'

She stepped forward and pressed the tin firmly on to Mr Scarecrow's head. It was a very *hard* head, and felt exactly like a turnip, only she didn't like to say so.

The tin was a perfect fit. She pulled the hinged lid over his eyes, and he looked for all the world like a soldier from Her Majesty's Grenadier Guards. You wouldn't really have noticed any difference, save that he had only a single leg.

The Little Dressmaker was impressed. 'It *does* suit him,' she agreed, coming up the path. 'And I expect it'll help to keep the birds away, too. They'll be frightened of the sunlight shining on the tin.'

She was perfectly right. The birds did not

come to steal seeds from the allotments any more. They could not make out what had come over Mr Scarecrow. He looked as real as anything. Why, he might even be carrying a gun! And when it rained, the drops made a loud, pattering noise on the tin hat. It was enough to frighten anybody. Except the robins. They enjoyed their privacy, and sang more loudly than ever.

The vegetables ripened quickly. The Little Dressmaker told Ragdolly Anna that when she could see a good-sized radish shoulder peeping out of the earth, she could give it a tug.

Soon they were able to gather a whole bunch and take them home for tea. The White Cat sniffed haughtily. 'Not for me, thank you,' he mewed. 'Too indigestible. All right for *ordinary* digestions, I suppose. Mine is an extraordinary one. But don't let me put you off.'

Dummy gazed at the radishes as if she admired them, and would have liked a taste. Ragdolly Anna waited until no one was looking. She chose a fine red one, dipped it in the salt, and held it to Dummy's delicately embroidered mouth.

There was a hardly-to-be-noticed nibble.

It was gone.

'If you can manage as well as *that*,' whispered Ragdolly Anna in Dummy's ear, 'one of these days we'll invite Mr Scarecrow to tea.'

And I am sure that Dummy flushed a little with pleasure, and her lips trembled into an almost-smile.

Ragdolly Anna
and the Pumpkin

*

The Little Dressmaker was pouring out her morning cup of tea. 'Ragdolly Anna . . .' she said, not too loudly, in case Ragdolly Anna was still asleep, but loud enough to break into her dream and tell her it was time to get up.

Ragdolly Anna turned over. She opened her eyes. For a moment she wasn't quite sure where she was. The Little Dressmaker had drawn back the curtains, and a mellow, glittering sunlight flooded the room five floors up. Lower down, the flats were still shadowed by the leaves of the tree which grew outside . . . but *they* were too high up for that. Dummy's head shone as if she wore a halo. 'Like a saint in a church window,' thought Ragdolly Anna; and the White Cat was stretched out to his full length on the window-seat, purring.

'The sunlight is the colour of lemon curd, isn't

it?' said the Little Dressmaker. 'Yellow gold. It'll be Harvest Festival this week. You'll see the children going by with their baskets, if you look out. Such a lovely morning! It's cold, though. What a good job I finished your autumn skirt yesterday, Ragdolly Anna. You can wear it today.'

The new skirt was hanging on the bedpost. It was made of brown corduroy velvet and had a pattern of tiny pink and yellow flowers, with leaves twined among them. Ragdolly Anna turned round in front of the glass. She thought she looked lovely – especially with her hat on.

'Some people,' commented the White Cat sleepily, 'are vain. I don't say everybody, mind. But some. Self respect is one thing ... vanity another. I dare say you'll grow out of it.' He stretched himself out another couple of inches. There was hardly room for anyone else on the window-seat at all. But when she had finished her breakfast, Ragdolly Anna managed to fit herself into the corner – just.

It was a new seat, with a red cushion on it and a bit of crochet on top of the cushion to stop the sun from fading it. Ragdolly Anna thought it was the best place of all to settle for an hour or so. It was like having a seat in a theatre. All sorts of things happened down below, and she could look at them and tell Dummy what was going on. Sometimes Dummy would be turned round, so that she could watch too.

The Little Dressmaker was nervous about windows. She had fixed some wooden bars across so that people couldn't possibly fall out – or even lean over, come to that. 'You have to use some common sense,' she had explained as she had hammered in the bars, occasionally banging her thumb by mistake, 'and never take risks with windows.'

'Risks,' interrupted the White Cat, 'are only taken by fools. There are a great many fools around.' He looked at Ragdolly Anna, and at Dummy too, with his blue eyes. 'I mention no names ... *That* is why it is necessary to Take Precautions.'

Ragdolly Anna wondered what precautions were – she hadn't seen any about – but the Little Dressmaker told her he only meant that it was sensible to be careful.

'And we all know *that*,' she said.

Today, in Harvest Thanksgiving Week, it was easy to see that something special was happening. The children running to school carried boxes and baskets as well as their satchels. Some of the boxes were crammed with pears and apples; some had grapes; a few were heaped with

vegetables of one kind and another; and there
was one little boy who bore an enormous
pumpkin.

The pumpkin was so big, he could hardly see
where he was going. Ragdolly Anna watched
him trying to keep up with the others. She felt
nervous.

'I hope he'll take Precautions,' she whispered
under her breath.

'Eh?' grunted the White Cat. 'Who? What?
Speak up, can't you?'

'I hope he'll . . .' Ragdolly Anna put her hand
to her mouth with a gasp. There was a scuffle

. . . a thump . . . a crash . . . Somebody cried out. Then came a noise of feet running away. And sobs.

It all happened so quickly that it was over almost as soon as it had started, and when the Little Dressmaker came to the window most of the children had disappeared round the corner.

Only the boy who had been carrying the pumpkin was left. He was sitting on the edge of the pavement, rubbing his knee. A trickle of blood made its way down his sock, and the big pumpkin lay in the gutter with a gash out of its side. It was spoiled.

'Oh!' cried out Ragdolly Anna. 'What a *shame*! They pushed him. I saw them! The big boys pushed him over and he fell down.'

'It is what we call Spite,' explained the White Cat, sitting up severely. 'Spite and Envy. They wished it was *their* pumpkin, I suppose. That's human nature. Now, we cats − we wouldn't be so silly. Whoever saw cats fighting over a pumpkin! Pumpkins, *indeed*!'

'You're not very sympathetic,' objected Ragdolly Anna. Sympathetic was a new word. She had only just learned it, and she didn't think she would be able to *spell* it, however hard she tried.

A big tear ran down Dummy's face, and fell

on to the carpet with a plop. 'Oh dear,' sighed the Little Dressmaker anxiously. 'I'm ever so busy this morning – I have to go to the dentist at nine. Somebody should run down and comfort that little boy, and bind up his knee, but I really haven't time. Could *you* go?' she asked the White Cat. 'You're so clever. You'd know what to do.'

'Cleverness is one thing; binding up knees is another,' replied the White Cat haughtily. 'I'll give directions, if you like. Instructions in First Aid. I did a Red Cross course once,' he added modestly, 'in my spare time. But I don't care for boys. Let *her* go. And bring him up.' He hunched his shoulders and glinted at Ragdolly Anna.

'By herself? She's not very big.' The Little Dressmaker looked anxious. She often looked anxious, and a thin, wrinkly line came over her forehead at such moments. When she laughed, the line went, and some small, crinkly ones came at the corners of her eyes instead.

'I'm quite big enough,' replied Ragdolly Anna. She drew herself up to her full height. She measured exactly 18 inches on one side of the tape, and 46 cm on the other.

'Well . . . maybe you could manage. Be *careful*. Go down *slowly*, or you'll have a tumble, too.

I'll leave the bandages on the table,' chattered the Little Dressmaker, 'and there's some ointment . . . and a safety pin. Make sure you wash the knee well first!' she called out just as she was closing the door. 'I'll be back later. Goodbye!'

She slipped into the lift and pressed the button. Down, down, down it went. When it got to the ground floor Ragdolly Anna and the White Cat heard a click. A minute or two later, the Little Dressmaker emerged. She looked up, and waved to them . . . then she bent for a moment and spoke a few words to the boy, who was trying to wipe the mud off the pumpkin . . . and hurried off. One must never be late for the dentist.

Ragdolly Anna felt important. She put her apron on, the one with a red cross stitched on the bib, because she didn't want to get blood on her new skirt. She pushed a stool to the sink, so that she could reach the tap, and filled a basin with warm water.

'Look out, can't you!' mewed the White Cat, as a trickle splashed his fur. He licked it, furiously. 'I'd better come with you, I suppose. There'll be accidents if I don't. You *are* my responsibility, while she's away. And you have a habit of getting into difficulties.'

'That's good! We can bring the boy up

between us,' commented Ragdolly Anna cheerfully. She went to the window, climbed on to the seat, and whistled.

It was rather a muffled kind of whistle, as she had only been practising whistling for quite a short time, and it came out in spurts which sounded a bit like a train going through a tunnel; but the boy heard it, and stopped sniffing, and looked up.

'We're coming to get you!' called Ragdolly Anna. 'See?'

His mouth dropped open.

Ragdolly Anna couldn't manage the lift by herself, but the White Cat reached a paw up and pressed the button which said Ground Floor, and they were down in no time.

'If you'll venture up to the fifth floor, young man,' invited the White Cat, swishing his tail a little because he wasn't terribly fond of boys, 'my small friend here will attend to your wound. If wound it is,' he added, peering closely with his bright blue eyes. 'It looks like a mere scratch to me.'

'It needs washing,' pronounced Ragdolly Anna. Seen from close up, the boy wasn't *quite* so big as she had imagined, but he was quite big enough. About seven years old, she guessed, in human reckoning. It was different for dollies, of course. Some dollies lived for *hundreds* of years, and might take a long, long time to grow up. 'What's your name?' she asked kindly.

'He'd better have a form to fill in,' whispered the White Cat, as they were all three going up in the lift again. It was fortunate it was working, for once. 'Stating his name, age, size, width, height, address, destination, occupation, and peregrination. Can you write?' he enquired sharply.

'I can write my name, of course. It's Sam. But I don't know all the other things,' answered the boy. 'I *can* hear what you're saying, you know. My word! What a jolly flat! Who's that, over there, with the dress on?'

'That's Dummy. She's my best friend,' said Ragdolly Anna.

'She doesn't talk much. Can she say hullo?'

Ragdolly Anna was bathing his knee, and it hurt a bit. It was better to look at something else while she was doing it. Sam cast his eyes round . . . then they came back to Dummy again. She wore her almost-smile, and a pale blue muslin party gown with gold stars on the bodice. It was only half finished, but she looked lovely.

'Cor! She's a smart one!' said Sam.

The White Cat had retired to the airing cup-

board, for he disliked the sight of blood. He was reading instructions from his First Aid book, propped up against some towels, and calling them out to Ragdolly Anna.

'After cleansing the wound, apply a dressing and a soft bandage,' he called. 'Are you giving me your attention? I'm only trying to make you a bit more clever . . .'

'I've *done* that! A dressing, and a bandage,' answered Ragdolly Anna proudly. 'And it's fastened with a safety pin. How does that feel?'

Sam stood up and straightened his leg gingerly. Then he tried walking round the room . . . first with a stiff knee . . . and then with a knee not *quite* so stiff . . . and then, suddenly, just like an ordinary boy.

'It's better!'

'Now for the pumpkin!' Ragdolly Anna had been a bit worried about that. Sam had carried it in his arms all the way up, and now it sat on the floor beside him. Most of it was all right. But there was a narrow gash in the side, which went right through to the middle. As if it had fallen on a stone.

They looked.

Sam's mouth began to droop. 'I can't take it to school like that. Not for the Harvest Festival.'

The White Cat drew in his breath. 'Where

there's a will there's a way,' he said. 'You've heard that, I take it? In simple language, a hole in a pumpkin means a *space* for something. Do I make myself clear?'

'A space for *what*?'

'Anything you fancy,' he went on carelessly. 'Anything ... I would put a candle in it, myself.'

'A candle?' At first, Ragdolly Anna was puzzled. Then Sam gave a hoot.

'Of course!' he shouted – so loudly, that Dummy jumped, and one of her stars slipped half an inch down her bodice. 'Like the candles we have in turnips, on Bonfire Night? A pumpkin candle? What a splendid idea!'

'Don't mention it,' mewed the White Cat graciously. 'Just came into my head, in passing, so to speak. If you get my meaning.'

'There's a candle by my bed,' said Ragdolly Anna excitedly. 'In a saucer. You can have that.'

They looked. Sure enough, there was a nightlight candle, a short, fat one, by the bed. Ragdolly Anna liked to keep one handy, in case she had a bad dream in the dark. But she hadn't had a bad dream for ages, and at 18 inches tall she had almost grown out of nightlights.

They scooped a little of the pumpkin flesh out with a teaspoon and made a tiny cave inside.

The candle sat in the cave. It was a perfect fit, and the gash in the side would make a miniature window for it to shine through.

'It's fantastic!' Sam held the pumpkin up with both hands. 'I'll show it to the lady ... What do you think of *that*, eh?'

Dummy hadn't got a very loud voice, you remember. In fact, I am not sure whether she had a voice at all. But I am *quite* sure her eyebrows moved, just a tiny bit, and her smile was a little wider than usual.

'I must hurry. I'll be late if I stay.' Sam stopped with one hand on the door handle. 'It

was ever so kind of you to help me. Thanks.'

They pulled back the heavy lift door and nudged him inside. Then they closed it.

'Push the bottom button,' hinted Ragdolly Anna.

The lift began to drop downwards.

'Goodbye!' called a faint voice from within. 'Goodbye!'

Quite soon after that, the Little Dressmaker returned from the dentist. She held her handkerchief to her lips; but her eyes were bright. She couldn't talk much at first, but she felt better when she had had a cup of tea. As she sipped it, she listened to their story.

'A candle?' she cried, joyfully, when they had finished. 'That's the best possible thing you could have thought of. I hope they light it when he gets to school!'

That evening, as dusk fell, they were just going to draw the curtains over when there was a whistle from below.

'Hullo?'

'It's Sam!' cried Ragdolly Anna. 'What happened?' she called excitedly. 'Did they light the candle?'

'They put the pumpkin on top of all the other boxes and baskets, and yes, it had a light inside it all the morning!' shouted Sam. 'Tomorrow it's to be sliced up – you might get some, if you're lucky!'

He hurried on home, for his elder sister had come to meet him and she was holding his hand.

'I wonder what he means by that?' mused the Little Dressmaker. 'I wonder!'

I believe that Ragdolly Anna dreamed of pumpkins that night. She dreamed they were all invited to a Pumpkin Party ... and everybody had slices of pumpkin pie to eat. So when Sam stopped and whistled under the window when he came out of school the next afternoon, and called that there was a parcel on the step, she wasn't surprised to find four large slices of pumpkin wrapped in coloured paper.

'For the people who live in the Flat on the Fifth Floor,' it said on the label. 'With love from Sam.'

So they had a whole slice each.

I never discovered whether Dummy ate hers, or not. The Little Dressmaker cut it up small and left it on a china plate beside her, in case she felt hungry. She forgot all about it when she went to bed; and in the morning, the plate was empty.

Of course, it *may* have been mice.

Dummy
Has an Adventure

*

It was autumn.

The Little Dressmaker stood by the window, five floors up, sipping her first cup of tea and looking down, down, down at the top of the plane tree which grew by the kerb. There was only one tree, because they lived in a town, but she had shown it to Ragdolly Anna when she had been quite small and learning about the names of things. Ragdolly Anna had looked down too, and admired the colour of the leaves – especially in spring. Then, when they were going shopping, she had looked up. The leaves appeared quite different from underneath. The light shone through them, and she had invented games, threading a path in and out of their shadows.

Now they were falling. Indeed, there were hardly any left. A Roadman came along with a barrow every morning and took the leaves away to burn them. Sometimes he waved to Ragdolly Anna.

Soon it would be Bonfire Night.

'Will we have fireworks?' asked Ragdolly Anna. She remembered seeing long streamers of fire shooting across the sky on the Fifth of November last year. There had been a public display in the recreation ground, but she had been too young to go. The Little Dressmaker had tucked her up in bed and left the curtain drawn aside a little bit. She had lain there, quite still, and watched . . .

This year, the Little Dressmaker promised her, they would go together. Dummy would stay behind to keep house, for she did not like to go out after dark; and the White Cat himself would remain with her for company.

'As long as there's no fog,' promised the Little Dressmaker, 'we'll wrap up warm – and go. Not if there's fog, mind. But I've plenty to do before then. I want to wash those curtains before winter sets in. We'll stand Dummy out in the corridor for the morning; then I can get on without knocking her over.'

She put on her big apron and rolled up her sleeves. Ragdolly Anna explained to Dummy

what was happening. She didn't seem to mind.
She had her almost-smile on her face, as though
she quite liked the idea of waiting in the corridor.
They pushed and pulled her, gently, and the
White Cat went in front to open the door.

Dummy leaned up against the wall. She only
had a sheet round her, to keep off the dust, for
the Little Dressmaker had just cut out a lady's
dressing gown and had been too busy to fit it
on yet.

There were other things piled outside the
doors of people who had flats in the same

building: odds and ends, mostly – tatters and rags. Nothing so big as Dummy.

'I expect there's a rummage collection for Guy Fawkes,' explained the Little Dressmaker.

'Guy Fawkes?'

'He tried to burn the Houses of Parliament, you know – but he didn't succeed.'

The White Cat looked over his shoulder. 'It's what we call Political Intrigue,' he drawled. 'History, you understand. History.'

'Oh,' said Ragdolly Anna.

That morning they worked hard. Ragdolly Anna had learned to polish. She had a special way of polishing the floor: she would put both feet on a large duster and slide from one end of the room to the other. It worked beautifully, and soon there was a splendid glow. The Little Dressmaker washed the curtains, and rubbed the window pane with a leather cloth. She hung up a bit of winter velvet, instead of the flowered cotton. It was old, but it looked warm and cosy, and they believed that Dummy would enjoy the extra privacy and freedom from draughts.

Then they called out that they were ready, and went to fetch her from the corridor. Their mouths fell open in astonishment.

'Oh!' they gasped.

There was nobody there. All the little bundles of rags and tatters had disappeared and Dummy had gone too.

'What *can* have happened?' asked the Little Dressmaker anxiously. 'She *never* wanders off by herself. Somebody must have taken her.'

'Dummy! Dummy!' called Ragdolly Anna. 'Where are you?'

There was no reply.

'Somebody should inquire,' mewed the White Cat. 'Somebody of significance ... Me! I will.'

He walked gracefully up to the doors of the other flats, and pressed the bells.

'My apologies for troubling you,' he began, 'but can you give me any information? Dummy has disappeared!'

Nobody could. Some of the flat-owners protested that they had been busy washing up, or making the beds, when the rummage collectors had come round. They had not seen Dummy at all, and could not imagine what had happened to her.

One thin man shut the door firmly, and then opened it again and put his thin nose through the crack.

'If you ask *me*,' he offered, 'they've taken her for a Guy. She'll be put on the bonfire, come the Fifth of November, and burned. Ha ha! What a joke.'

He shut the door again with a click, and they could hear him laughing behind it.

The Little Dressmaker threw her apron over her head and burst into tears. But she didn't cry for long. She blew her nose on a pink tissue, and then on a yellow one.

'Put on your hat, Ragdolly Anna,' she instructed, straightening her back. 'We'll go along to the recreation ground and find out. They'll be making the Guy there, in the pavilion. We'll soon discover what's happened.'

'It may be too late,' said the White Cat gloomily. 'Or too early,' he added. He took a few laps of milk from his saucer. 'But it may not. That is what we call Philosophy.'

He strolled slowly, very slowly, over to the window-sill, and sat up, stiff as a wooden spoon, by the velvet curtain.

'I shall keep a look out,' he said.

Ragdolly Anna put on her hat and her woollen shawl, for it was getting chilly. The Little Dressmaker took her umbrella. It was not raining, but you never knew when an umbrella might be useful. If there were fights, she could thump the ringleaders on the head with it.

'Fights?' questioned Ragdolly Anna.

She felt a bit nervous. But with her hat pulled well down over her ears, and a big bunch of roses on the brim, somehow or other her courage returned to her. They set off cheerfully, holding hands, in the direction of the recreation ground.

A mile is a long way when you are not very tall. Ragdolly Anna settled into a sort of jog-trot, to keep up with the Little Dressmaker. She was out of breath by the time they reached the big iron gates of the recreation ground. There was the pavilion, and a noise of chatter and laughter came from it. Something was going on. Should they knock?

They knocked. But there was so much clamour that no one heard them. They opened the door and stepped inside.

What a tumultuous scene! It took the Little Dressmaker a moment or two to take it in. Boxes of fireworks here, boxes of fireworks there – rockets and Golden Rain, Roman Candles and squibs all jostling each other, being kept safe and dry ready for the Fifth of November. Piles of rummage: rags, old plimsolls, worn out waistcoats and tatty scarves – all for dressing the Guy. Everywhere there were children (quite *big* children; I suspect they were teenagers) busily doing something to somebody who was to sit on top of the bonfire wearing a Guy Fawkes hat.

It wasn't a scarecrow. It wasn't a kitchen mop, with string for hair and a cushion for a stomach. It wasn't even a sackful of straw with eyes and a nose sewn on to the slimmest end.

It was Dummy!

Poor Dummy! She had lost the sheet which had been wrapped round her to keep the dust away. She was wearing a dirty, torn singlet. They had tied a scarf with moth holes in it round her neck, and were actually fixing on a false nose with a piece of elastic. Her eyes were open, but she didn't give her almost-smile any more. The corners of her beautifully designed mouth were turned down ever so slightly . . . She would have wept, if she had known how.

'Stop! Stop!' cried the Little Dressmaker. 'What are you doing?'

'We're making a Guy, out of the rummage from the flats,' answered a boy, grinning. 'See this? We found it on the landing, on the fifth floor. This'll light beautifully. You can bet your boots it will. What a bit of luck!'

'*That* is not rummage!' insisted the Little Dressmaker in authoritative tones. 'That is *Dummy*! Give her back *at once*. She belongs to *us*.'

She waved her umbrella; and for a moment it seemed that Dummy recognized her rescuers,

for her lips seemed to move a little to suggest the shadow of an almost-smile.

'*My*! That *is* a mistake, and no mistake!' commented the boy in astonishment. 'You're only just in time. We'll have to make another Guy Fawkes, won't we?'

'What did I tell you, Sammy?' said his friend. 'I told you it was too fine for rummage. *That's* not rummage, I said. It's a dummy that belongs to the Little Dressmaker. Give it to her back.'

You can imagine how pleased Dummy was to be with Ragdolly Anna and the Little Dressmaker again. The only difficulty was – how were they to get her all the way home? It was at least a mile to the Flat on the Fifth Floor; and Dummy had no legs.

'We'll telephone to the White Cat,' decided the Little Dressmaker. '*He'll* advise us. He loves giving advice, and he always knows what is the best thing to do.'

So while Ragdolly Anna stayed close to Dummy, in case she should feel she had been deserted, the Little Dressmaker marched off to the local telephone box and put a call through to the White Cat.

'Hullowwww?' he answered, in his most dignified manner. 'This is the Flat on the Fifth Floor. Can I help you?'

'We've found Dummy.' (The Little Dress-maker spoke as quickly as she could, for she hadn't many coppers in her purse and telephone calls were expensive.) 'She's at the recreation ground. How shall we get her home?'

'By wheelbarrow, of course,' said the White Cat sharply. 'The old fellow down below, sweeping up the leaves. I'll tell him. He's got an *enormous* barrow. Most useful. Most opportune. Goodbye!'

He rang off. The telephone gave a curt tinkle, and was silent.

The Little Dressmaker hurried back to the pavilion. Dummy was being prepared for her journey. They had tidied her up and dressed her in a large floral gown with rhododendrons on it, which had turned up in the rummage. It really suited her. And they had hardly finished admiring it when the Roadman trundled up with his barrow. There was *plenty* of room for Dummy in it, and for Ragdolly Anna too.

They returned home in splendid style. The Little Dressmaker was so grateful to the Road-man for his help that she invited him in for tea.

'We're dreadfully hungry,' she said. 'We've had hardly anything to eat all day. *Do* come in. We'll have boiled eggs, and I'll open a tin of peaches. And cream.'

'Peaches?' questioned the White Cat. 'A good idea. *You* have the peaches. *I'll* have the cream.'

One always feels better when one has eaten a little bit of something. After their meal they gave the Roadman an extra jam sandwich to put in his pocket for supper, and waved him good-bye.

'It was a horrifying adventure,' repeated the Little Dressmaker, several times, opening her eyes so wide that the crinkles nearly disappeared. 'It will teach us to be more careful in future. *Anything* might be taken away for rummage. *You*

74

might,' she told Ragdolly Anna. 'Or *I* might – if I were to fall asleep one morning on the doorstep. *He* might –'

'There is not the slightest possibility that anyone would mistake me for rummage,' broke in the White Cat, haughtily. 'Speak for yourselves!'

That night they all went to bed early and slept well.

It wasn't long before Firework Day really came: fine, clear and frosty. There was no fog.

'Can we go to the recreation ground bonfire?' asked Ragdolly Anna, trembling with excitement.

The Little Dressmaker thought they might. They waited until it was almost dusk, and then put on an extra pair of socks each and two pairs of gloves and a great number of shawls and cardigans and mufflers. Ragdolly Anna wore her straw hat with the paper roses on it, and a pixie hood on top of that. Indeed, they had so many clothes on that when the time came for them to set out they found the greatest difficulty in moving at all.

The White Cat settled himself for the evening by the velvet curtain, and peered down at them curiously. 'Extraordinary!' he purred. 'But they mean well. After all, they are only human – and one of them is not even that.' He closed his eyes.

The bonfire at the recreation ground was so big that they felt themselves warmed by the glow of it when they were quite a long way off. And the fireworks! Ragdolly Anna had never seen such a tumble of purple, emerald and gold; they burst in glittering cascades all over the night sky. She could not decide which she liked best. Rockets were inclined to be frightening – they were in such a hurry to be off and they made a noise like an express train when they were lighted! Golden Rain took her to Fairyland – although it ceased just as she was in the middle of enjoying it. She liked the splutter of Flower Pots, and the little red and purple Bengal Lights. Most magical of all, perhaps, were the Roman Candles. They burned steadily for a time, and then – just as she had given up expecting any-thing – they seemed to loosen, and sent up a clear and lovely star. Sometimes it was green, and sometimes pink or violet.

Long after the display was ended, when they had walked home, marvelling, and had sipped a mug of cocoa to settle themselves, and had snuggled into bed, Ragdolly Anna's head was still full of lights and patterns.

As for Dummy, she had admired the display

from her position by the window, with the White Cat drowsily purring on one side of her and the velvet curtain on the other.

She was perfectly happy.

Ragdolly Anna's
Christmas

*

Ragdolly Anna liked Christmas. She started to think about it early, because then she could make it stretch out as long as possible. First, she thought of decorations. The Little Dressmaker always had some ideas about those.

'You could save the silver milk-bottle tops,' she suggested, 'and make chains with them. You only have to bore a hole in the middle, and they're quite easy to thread.'

So that was one thing.

Then there were fir cones. They often found a fir cone or two when they were walking in the park, and brought them home in case they might come in useful. Once, Ragdolly Anna had lost a fir cone somewhere on the allotments. She thought a squirrel must have taken it, for she never found it again. But by the time the evenings began to get shorter and darker they had collected quite a lot. Some of them they painted ... and some of them they piled in a bowl with a tangerine or two among them. Dummy gave her almost-smile when she saw the tangerines, for she knew that Christmas could not be very far away.

One evening, when they were cutting out some pictures from last year's cards and making new ones out of them, the Little Dressmaker told Ragdolly Anna the story of her first Christmas.

'You had only just been sewn up, and you hadn't learned to talk then or even to use your arms and legs. I had put you in a boot box for the night. Then, in the morning, there was nobody there! The box was empty!'

'Where was I?' asked Ragdolly Anna breathlessly.

'The mice had stolen you. We had a lot that winter. They had come into the cupboard under the stairs – for warmth, I dare say. They had dragged you down under the floorboards, and it was some days before you were found again. I *was* worried.'

'*I* found you,' added the White Cat. 'You should remember that! If it hadn't been for me ...'

Ragdolly Anna shuddered.

'There aren't any mice there now, love,' said

the Little Dressmaker comfortingly. 'And even if there were, you could easily run off. You've learned a great many things since those days.'

'True,' agreed the White Cat. 'But there's plenty more to learn. What about Long Division, Short Division, or even Multiplication? What about ice-skating, roller-skating, or raffia work? She can't do *any* of that, can she? She can't fly ... she can't swim ... she can't ...'

'There are a great number of things she *can* do,' interrupted the Little Dressmaker briskly. 'She's *very* good at sticking on stamps. There are eleven envelopes ready, Ragdolly Anna. Those are for my customers, the people I sew for during the year. Will you seal them up for me? But I've only got six stamps.'

Ragdolly Anna sealed the envelopes, and fixed a stamp on the top right-hand corner of the first six. Even the White Cat could find nothing wrong with them.

'Not bad, not bad at all,' he said graciously, waving his tail. 'And now I suppose you'll be off to the Post Office.'

'That's exactly were we *are* going,' said the Little Dressmaker. 'And we may be a long time. They're busy this week. I expect there will be a queue.'

'That's funny,' said Ragdolly Anna as they

went off. 'I know Q comes after P and before R, but what's it doing in the Post Office?'

The Little Dressmaker explained, while they hurried with their envelopes, that a queue was a different thing from a 'Q', and all she meant was that there might be a long, long line of people, all wishing to post things. They would have to wait for their turn.

There *was* an extremely long line, but Ragdolly Anna was pleased. While the Little Dressmaker took her place in the queue, she could wander round, looking at the decorations. For the Post Office was quite transfigured.

Twisted chains of shiny, coloured paper hung from corner to corner. Some were like necklaces, some were cut into fantastic shapes. Here and there a paper bell was suspended, red, green, white or yellow. There were angels cut out of gold stuff, and tiny striped birds. There were wreaths of holly and mistletoe, freckled with candles. Best of all, she thought, were the Christmas trees. There were six or seven of them, and from their spread branches hung balls, stars, diamonds, trumpets, bells, flowers, and miniature toys of every imaginable kind. Tinsel and icicles quivered on the trees, and on the top of each was poised something special: a fairy doll, pink and glittering ... an angel ... or an enormous star. They were *very* expensive.

It was while Ragdolly Anna was staring up at these that she heard someone say: 'How much is the rag dolly, please?' and felt herself being picked up by an assistant she hadn't met before and balanced among the branches of the tallest tree.

'Oh dear ... Oh dear ... Oh dear. I mustn't be frightened,' she whispered to herself, 'but I do hope I shan't fall off. And I hope the Little Dressmaker will catch sight of me!'

But the Little Dressmaker was busy counting out her stamp money, and wasn't looking.

'I never saw a fairy doll with a big straw hat on before,' complained somebody. 'It looks odd.'

'Maybe it's an angel?' suggested another voice.

'*That's* not an angel,' scoffed a third. 'It's got no wings. I know an angel when I see one, any day.'

'Can we buy it, Mum?' asked a child, tugging her mother's skirt. 'Can we take it home?'

Ragdolly Anna trembled. 'You can't buy me,' she whispered. 'I'm *real!*' But nobody heard.

'We'll ask the shop assistant about it,' answered the lady, 'but it might have got into the wrong place. It doesn't look like a decoration, does it? It's wearing a petticoat and bloomers, and it's got a purse round its neck with proper money in it!'

'And a shawl!' called somebody else. 'You don't find people with *shawls* on Christmas trees – or only by accident. I'm going to lift it off!'

Ragdolly Anna did not like having so many eyes fastened on her at once, but she *did* like the young man who lifted her down and straightened her hat and her shawl. She had often seen him before, delivering parcels. Sometimes he had come into the kitchen of the Flat on the Fifth Floor and sat down to a hot drink and a ginger biscuit. Surely *he* would recognize

her! He would know that she was not for sale.

'I'm a real person,' she whispered, as his great hand clasped her gently and lifted her from the branches.

'Blow me down if it isn't Ragdolly Anna from the top-floor flat! You'll get yourself wrapped up, if you don't watch out, young lady. Where's the Little Dressmaker?'

'There she is!' cried Ragdolly Anna with relief. 'Searching for me, I expect. We've brought our Christmas letters.'

'You're just in time for the post, then!' The young man smiled and waved, as he went off with his sack to empty the box. But the Little Dressmaker was looking troubled.

'Where have you been, for goodness' sake?' she questioned. 'On the *Christmas* tree? I never heard of such a thing! It's important not to be sold,' she warned Ragdolly Anna. 'After all, you're not an ordinary toy; you're *nearly* human – and not everybody knows about that. You'll have to keep closer to me in future ... at least until Christmas is over. We don't want an accident.'

They soon forgot about the anxieties of the morning. But Ragdolly Anna could not get the Christmas trees out of her head. She wished they could buy one – but they cost far too much money. It seemed they would have to do the best they could with a few loose branches. The Little Dressmaker arranged them tastefully in a pot, and hung baubles on them. That was certainly a pretty sight. She stood the pot on the table, so that Dummy could enjoy it too.

It was when they were getting ready for bed that Ragdolly Anna remembered Mr Scarecrow. They couldn't send him a card, she thought, because he didn't live in a house and he hadn't got a letter-box. But they could take him something for a present. Not chocolate, for he hadn't a tooth for sweets. Not slippers, for he was dug well into the ground and wouldn't need them. Not a ball, because his arms were straight and stiff. A scarf! A new scarf would be a *splendid* present! And Ragdolly Anna could knit it herself in a day or two, for she had learned something called French knitting that you did with a cotton reel, lifting the stitches over nails fixed in the top with a hook, and pulling the knitting through the hole. 'I *can* do French knitting,' she murmured drowsily. 'He'll like that.'

In the morning, as soon as they had cleared away their breakfast, she settled herself on a chair and began. The scarf grew and grew. It was made of bits and bobs that had been left over from other things, and the colours merged into each other wonderfully. Every now and again Ragdolly Anna gave the scarf a tug, to make it seem longer. It was soon *so* long that it reached from one end of the table to the other. When the last fragment of wool was finished, she came to a full stop.

'That a scarf?' questioned the White Cat. He raised one eyebrow. 'A bit common, isn't it? A bit loud? I don't fancy bright colours myself. I always wear white ... you may have noticed. White fur.'

But the Little Dressmaker praised Ragdolly

Anna for her work. She was sure Mr Scarecrow would be delighted. Indeed, it was only just finished in time; and the week before Christmas they wrapped it up and carried it round to the allotment together with a small bottle of home-made wine.

Mr Scarecrow was singing softly to himself. 'It keeps me heart up, see?' he explained. 'It keeps me lungs in good order. And Christmas is a cold time for scarecrows.

> 'There ain't no seeds a-planting,
> there b'ain't no birds to scare,
> there ain't no diggers digging –
> there's only scarecrows there!

'You gotta laugh! But things'll get better.'

The Little Dressmaker took the cork out of the bottle and tipped an inch or two of the home-made wine down his throat. He smacked his lips, and Ragdolly Anna watched a flush of colour come back into his cheeks when he had swallowed it.

'Elderberry, ain't it? Good as a 'ot-water bottle,' he croaked, for his voice was a little husky. 'Please to open the parcel – I'm not very 'andy with knots. Ha ha! A joke, see? Nots . . . and knots! You get me?'

Ragdolly Anna unloosened the string and folded back the paper.

'What's that, then? A scarf? A muffler? Ain't it a lark, eh? All them colours. More like a rainbow than summat to wear. Let's 'ave it on!'

They wound the scarf around Mr Scarecrow's shoulders, over his plastic cape, and round his neck. It went round fifteen times before the end was reached. He looked fat and bonny, wearing it – quite a different sort of person.

Just as they were getting ready to go home, he gave a chuckle.

'I've got a surprise for you, too, I 'ave,' he told them. 'Look be'ind me! Go on – look!'

The Little Dressmaker had started on ahead, and heard nothing. But Ragdolly Anna crept behind Mr Scarecrow – and caught her breath.

There stood a perfect miniature Christmas tree. Exactly the right height for a small person. It was fresh and green and sturdy, and would look beautiful if it were decorated. It stood in a clay pot, and could be carried away. But where did it come from?

'Remember them fir cones?' Mr Scarecrow asked her. 'It wasn't this year, mind. It wasn't last year, neither . . . but *some* time you lost one on the allotment. You get me? Then comes a

squirrel . . . and 'e drops it in a flower pot. Then comes winter . . . and 'e forgets where 'e's put it. You still with me? There was a nice bit of soil in that there flower pot, nice and 'andy like. So you gets a fir tree. Surprised you, didn't I? Ha ha!'

Mr Scarecrow chuckled again, and tucked his chin into his scarf.

The miniature tree was quite heavy to carry in its pot, but Ragdolly Anna wanted it to be specially hers till it was dressed. She only just managed to get it home. And then the decorating began. There were some tiny bracelets which she had threaded once, when she had been ill – the beads were no bigger than hundreds and thousands. How lucky that she had saved them! The Little Dressmaker pressed some milk-bottle tops round her finger, and made bells . . . She screwed some rosettes out of toffee paper. And they came upon twelve old brass curtain rings which looked as if they were really gold when they were polished and hung upon the branches. But what should they put on top? It had to be something unusual.

'If I might make a suggestion,' broke in the White Cat. 'You could construct an original sort of star out of used matchsticks.'

'*Matchsticks*? How?' asked Ragdolly Anna.

'Arrange them crosswise ... tie them in the middle ... paint them silver (if you've got any paint). It's perfectly easy,' explained the White Cat graciously. 'Just a bit of imagination, you understand. Of course, you aren't an animal, are you? So not much is to be expected. But follow my instructions. I give them free, naturally – because it's Christmas.'

The Little Dressmaker found some used matchsticks in a saucer, quite long ones, and helped Ragdolly Anna arrange them crosswise. It was true – they soon began to look like stars, and you quickly forgot they had ever been matchsticks at all. When the tree was quite finished, they put it in the centre of the window-sill and left the curtains open a little bit. After it grew dusk, people hurrying home along the street below were attracted by an unusual bright-ness. Looking up, they saw a Christmas tree glowing from the window of the flat on the top floor – almost as if it were on fire. The lamp outside flung a beam directly towards it. It was as good as the big trees in the Post Office.

'Better,' whispered Ragdolly Anna to Dummy. 'Much, much better, isn't it?'

Dummy hadn't been to the Post Office, but she had watched the dressing of the little tree from its earliest beginning, and trembled with

an inward delight. You couldn't be surprised at
that, could you? For tomorrow, everybody knew,
it would really be Christmas.

*

RAGDOLLY ANNA
Jean Kenward

Although she's only made from a morsel of this and a tatter of that, Ragdolly Anna is a very special doll. And within hours of beginning to live with the little Dressmaker, the White Cat and Dummy, she embarks on some hair-raising adventures. Six delightful stories for children of five to seven.

LITTLE DOG LOST
Nina Warner Hooke

Pepito is a bright-eyed, cheerful little dog, with ears too big for his head and a funny short tail. He was born in an old cardboard box in a corner of a Spanish fruit market, but one fateful day he is separated from his mother and from then on he seems destined for travel and adventure. But will he ever find what he so yearns for – a *real* home?

DUCK BOY
Christobel Mattingley

The holiday at Mrs Perry's farm doesn't start very well for Adam.
His older brother and sister don't want to spend any time with him,
so he's bored and lonely. But then he discovers the creek and meets
two old ducks who obviously need some help. Every year their eggs
are stolen by rats or foxes, so Adam strikes a bargain with them:
he'll help guard their nest, they'll let him learn to swim in their
creek.

THE RAILWAY CAT
Phyllis Arkle

Alfie the railway cat lives at the station where he's a favourite with
all the regular passengers. The only trouble is that Hack, the new
Railway Porter, doesn't like cats and he soon has a plan for getting
rid of Alfie.

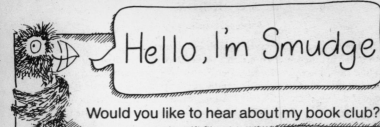

Hello, I'm Smudge

Would you like to hear about my book club?

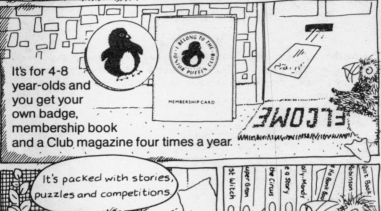

It's for 4-8 year-olds and you get your own badge, membership book and a Club magazine four times a year.

I BELONG TO THE JUNIOR PUFFIN CLUB

MEMBERSHIP CARD

ELCOME

It's packed with stories, puzzles and competitions.

The Egg

You get a chance to buy new books!

And there's lots more! For further details and an application form send a stamped, addressed envelope to:

The Junior Puffin Club,
Penguin Books Limited,
Bath Road,
Harmondsworth,
Middlesex UB7 0DA